D0587607

About the Author

The author is originally from the UK. He has a Japanese wife called Mika, and two boys, Kai and Seb. This is his second children's story after "Snowy the Zebra". The illustrations depict the family house and vicinity in Todoroki, Tokyo, and were done by Anna Yuki, a family friend. The story is about karma, which Seb learns about through his interactions with a friendly neighbourhood crow, he calls Christopher.

About the Illustrator

Anna Yuki – Swedish Japanese illustrator residing in Tokyo. Recently (2018) published a life style book, "Jibun o Itawaru Kurashigoto, Thoughts on Gentle Living", from K.K. Shufu to Seikatsusha Publishing. http://www.shufu.co.jp Instagram @ayukihouse

Written By
SIMON CHILDS

CHRISTOPHER
THE KARMA CROW

Illustrated by Anna Yuki

AUSTIN MACAULEY PUBLISHERS™
LONDON • CAMBRIDGE • NEW YORK • SHARJAH

A CIP catalogue record for this title is available from the British Library.

ISBN 9781788788960 (Paperback)
ISBN 9781788788977 (Hardback)
ISBN 9781788788984 (E-Book)

www.austinmacauley.com

First Published (2018)
Austin Macauley Publishers™ Ltd.
25 Canada Square
Canary Wharf
London
E14 5LQ

Dedication

To my second son, Seb

Seb lived with his mummy and
daddy and his big brother Kai, in
a house near a river, on a quiet
one-way street.

Some mornings, Seb was woken by
crows cawing as they looked for
left-over food in the street's litter bins.

Seb had a favourite crow he called Christopher. He was smaller than the others, and he had a white tuft of feathers on his head.

Christopher was the least shy, and he would often follow Seb when he left for school.

One day, Seb got back from school and saw that Christopher had hurt his leg and was hobbling. He saw some older boys running away with catapults in their hands, and he knew what had happened.

Seb and his mummy bandaged
Christopher up as best they could,
and fed him some bread and milk.
"Are you okay Christopher?"
asked Seb.
"Yes, thank you," said
Christopher. "I won't forget how
kind you have been to me."

Soon he was able to fly away, and
he circled overhead a few times to
show Seb how happy he was.

The next day, Seb went to school
again and was chased by
the same boys.

Suddenly, Christopher the crow
appeared as if from nowhere and
swooped down over the boys.
They stopped chasing Seb and
ran away as fast as they could!

Christopher managed to leave
some bird droppings on their
clothes and hair for good measure,
which made Seb giggle to see!

Seb told his daddy what happened
over dinner, and his daddy
explained that this was karma.
"If you do good things to
people, you can look forward to good
things in return, but if
you do bad things, bad things might
happen to you too."

After that, Seb called Christopher his
karma crow, and the two friends
often played hide and seek together.

Christopher the Karma Crow

This is the delightful story of a boy called Seb, and his interactions with a friendly neighbourhood crow in Tokyo, he calls Christopher. The story teaches us about karma, as Christopher dishes this out to two local bullies who pick on him and Seb.